MW00900019

Araviana and Alessio,
watching you grow is my greatest blessing.
You make me so proud.
Luke, I am grateful for every precious moment
and for your continuous support.

Thank you all for bringing so much
love and light into my life.

Copyright 2023 Adele Lamothe.
All rights reserved, including the right to reproduce this book
or portions thereof in any form whatsoever.

This book is written in American English.

Illustrations by Steven Tu

ISBN 978-1-7389434-3-2

TWO LITTLE RAINDROPS

Written by Adele Lamothe

Illustrated by Steven Tu

Two little friends,
tiny droplets so light,

lived in a cloud which
was puffy and white.

One was called Splish,
he had eyes like a fish,

and one was called Splash,
with a fancy mustache.

One day in Spring,
the friends were at play.

The sky became dark
and the clouds were all gray.

The friends felt so heavy and weak at the knees.
They battled to float so they had to break free.

They squeezed through the crowd and with a big sigh,
they jumped off the landing to soar through the sky.

They raced through the air, heading straight for the ground,
and landed on trees with a splishy-splash sound.

They felt a lot better, as light as can be,

but then they remembered, they missed family.

They started to worry as they looked around.
"How will we get home?"
they thought with a frown.

They slid down a leaf, landing high on a hill.
"We'll find a way home, together, we will!"

With a swish and a swoosh, they slipped down the peak.
"Look for some water, a stream we must seek!"

They dashed over grass and they whizzed past a rock, swerving around with a *kick* and a *knock*.

Faster and faster they moved with a thrill,
until they saw water - a stream on the hill.

Downhill they went, finding their way,
meeting the stream with a splash and a spray.

The stream was alive,
heading straight for the lake.

It flowed over stones,
with a rumble and shake.

The lake was right there and the droplets went plop!
Hitting the surface, they came to a stop.

Gone was the darkness and gray overhead.
The sky became bright and the sun shone instead.

The droplets relaxed as they drifted around.
The breeze was so warm, there was barely a sound.

The air became hot with the change in the weather.
The friends started feeling as light as a feather.

They started to *rise* as they turned into vapor,
and floated up higher than the biggest skyscraper.

They flew past a valley with fields in a row,
and soared over daisies as white as the snow.

It felt a lot colder up there in the sky.
They changed into water while floating up high.

So many new droplets were joining the pair.
They all formed a cloud - their whole family was there.

"We made it," they yawned, as they lay down their heads.
Tonight they'll sleep well in their soft, cozy beds.

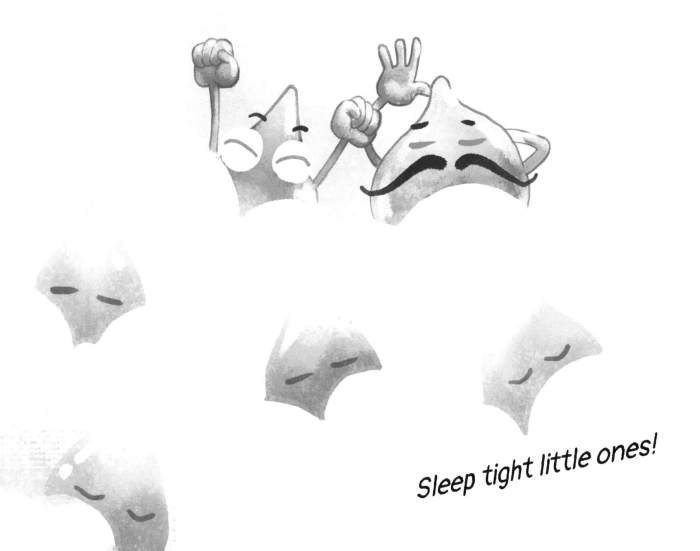

Sleep tight little ones!

The water cycle

When a cloud becomes full and heavy with tiny water droplets, the droplets fall from the sky as rain. We call this **precipitation**.

The rain falls to the ground, and runs downhill to form streams, lakes and oceans. When water droplets come together in one place, we call it **collection**.

Some rain lands on soil, where it is sucked up by roots, providing water to flowers and trees so that they can grow.

When the sun gets hot, droplets in streams, lakes and oceans float up into the air and become water vapor. We call this **evaporation**.

As the water vapor rises higher and higher, the cool air makes the vapor turn back into liquid water. This is called **condensation**. The droplets come together to form a cloud and the adventure starts all over again!

This is the path that water droplets follow as they move around the Earth. It is called **the water cycle**.

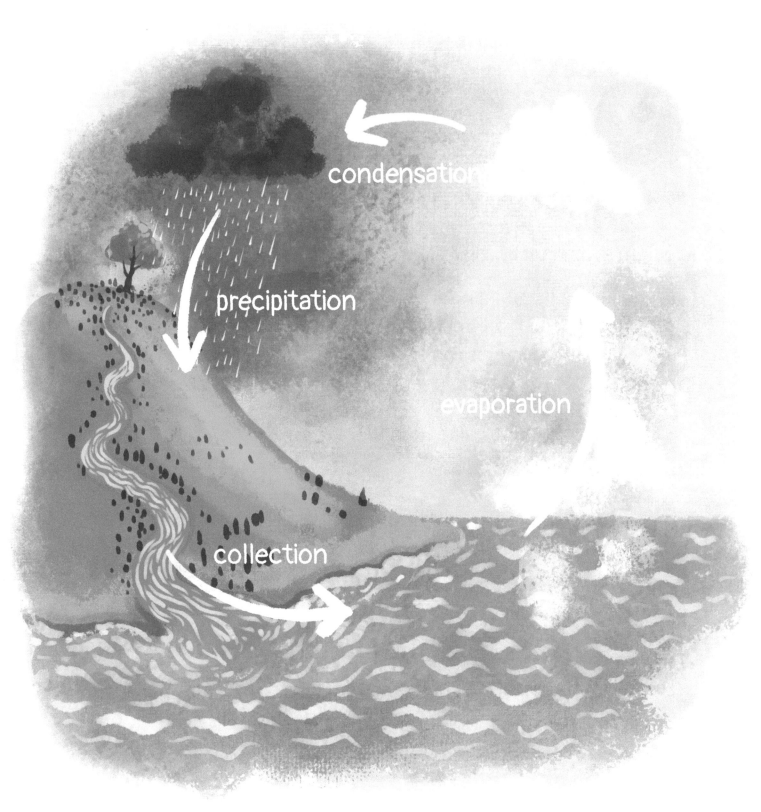

Every drop counts!

Water is needed by people, animals and plants. If we all use less water, there will be enough for every living thing.

You can save water by doing a few simple things each day:

 Turn off the tap while brushing your teeth

 If you see a tap leaking, tell someone who can get it fixed

 Take a shower instead of a bath

 Collect rainwater for the garden

Remember to keep water clean, which means no littering, especially in your local lakes, rivers and streams.

Thank you for reading 'Two Little Raindrops'!

I would love to know if you enjoyed this book. Please consider leaving an honest review on Amazon. It will mean so much, as you will be helping me on my journey as an author. You will also be helping other readers, as honest reviews help readers to find the right book for their needs.

With sincere thanks,

Adele

Printed in the USA
CPSIA information can be obtained
at www.ICGtesting.com
LVHW070943301023
762334LV00001B/13

Araviana and Alessio,
watching you grow is my greatest blessing.
You make me so proud.
Luke, I am grateful for every precious moment
and for your continuous support.

Thank you all for bringing so much
love and light into my life.

Copyright 2023 Adele Lamothe.
All rights reserved, including the right to reproduce this book
or portions thereof in any form whatsoever.

This book is written in American English.

Illustrations by Steven Tu

ISBN 978-1-7389434-3-2

TWO LITTLE RAINDROPS

Written by Adele Lamothe

Illustrated by Steven Tu

Two little friends,
tiny droplets so light,

lived in a cloud which
was puffy and white.

One was called Splish,
he had eyes like a fish,

and one was called Splash,
with a fancy mustache.

One day in Spring,
the friends were at play.

The sky became dark
and the clouds were all gray.

The friends felt so heavy and weak at the knees.
They battled to float so they had to break free.

They squeezed through the crowd and with a big sigh,
they jumped off the landing to soar through the sky.

They raced through the air, heading straight for the ground, and landed on trees with a splishy-splash sound.

They felt a lot better, as light as can be,

but then they remembered, they missed family.

They started to worry as they looked around.
"How will we get home?"
they thought with a frown.

They slid down a leaf, landing high on a hill.
"We'll find a way home, together, we will!"

With a swish and a swoosh, they slipped down the peak.
"Look for some water, a stream we must seek!"

They dashed over grass and they whizzed past a rock,
swerving around with a *kick* and a *knock*.

Faster and faster they moved with a thrill,
until they saw water - a stream on the hill.

Downhill they went, finding their way,
meeting the stream with a splash and a spray.

The stream was alive,
heading straight for the lake.

It flowed over stones,
with a rumble and shake.

The lake was right there and the droplets went plop!
Hitting the surface, they came to a stop.

Gone was the darkness and gray overhead.
The sky became bright and the sun shone instead.

The droplets relaxed as they drifted around.
The breeze was so warm, there was barely a sound.

The air became hot with the change in the weather.
The friends started feeling as light as a feather.

They started to ^{rise} as they turned into vapor,
and floated up higher than the biggest skyscraper.

They flew past a valley with fields in a row,
and soared over daisies as white as the snow.

It felt a lot colder up there in the sky.
They changed into water while floating up high.

So many new droplets were joining the pair.
They all formed a cloud - their whole family was there.

"We made it," they yawned, as they lay down their heads.
Tonight they'll sleep well in their soft, cozy beds.

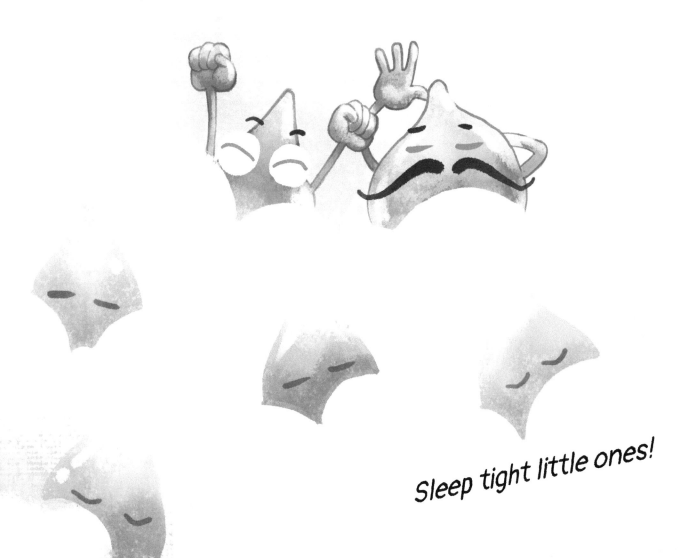

Sleep tight little ones!

The water cycle

When a cloud becomes full and heavy with tiny water droplets, the droplets fall from the sky as rain. We call this **precipitation**.

The rain falls to the ground, and runs downhill to form streams, lakes and oceans. When water droplets come together in one place, we call it **collection**.

Some rain lands on soil, where it is sucked up by roots, providing water to flowers and trees so that they can grow.

When the sun gets hot, droplets in streams, lakes and oceans float up into the air and become water vapor. We call this **evaporation**.

As the water vapor rises higher and higher, the cool air makes the vapor turn back into liquid water. This is called **condensation**. The droplets come together to form a cloud and the adventure starts all over again!

This is the path that water droplets follow as they move around the Earth. It is called **the water cycle**.

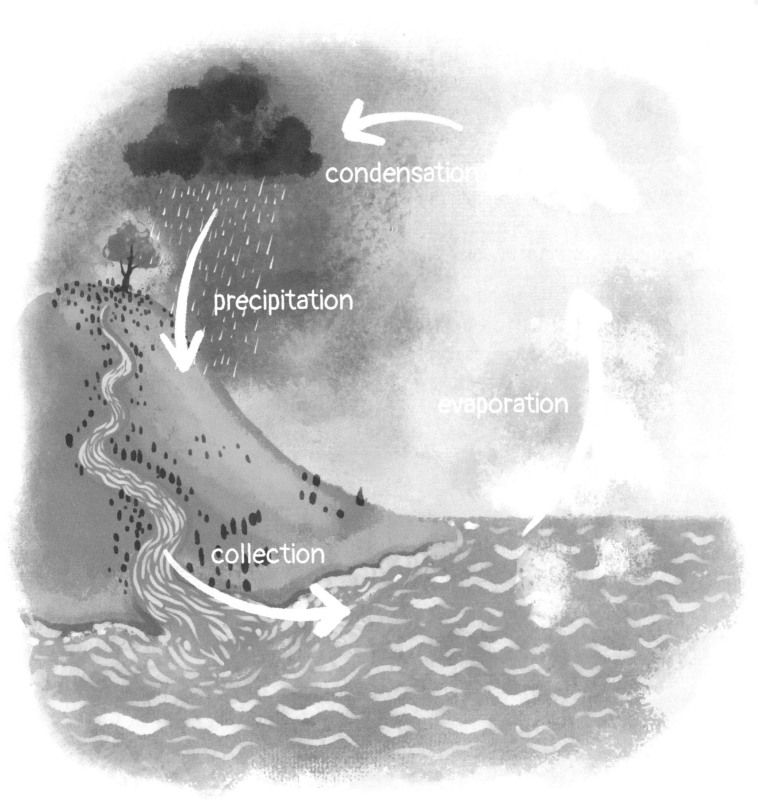

Every drop counts!

Water is needed by people, animals and plants. If we all use less water, there will be enough for every living thing.

You can save water by doing a few simple things each day:

 Turn off the tap while brushing your teeth

 If you see a tap leaking, tell someone who can get it fixed

 Take a shower instead of a bath

 Collect rainwater for the garden

Remember to keep water clean, which means no littering, especially in your local lakes, rivers and streams.

Thank you for reading 'Two Little Raindrops'!

I would love to know if you enjoyed this book. Please consider leaving an honest review on Amazon. It will mean so much, as you will be helping me on my journey as an author. You will also be helping other readers, as honest reviews help readers to find the right book for their needs.

With sincere thanks,

Adele

Printed in the USA
CPSIA information can be obtained
at www.ICGtesting.com
LVHW070943301023
762334LV00001B/13